Turtle Splash!

by
Cathryn Falwell

COUNTDOWN AT THE POND

GREENWILLOW BOOKS *An Imprint of HarperCollinsPublishers*

For the
residents of
Phinney Street
and the
inhabitants of
Frog Song Pond,
Gorham, Maine

Library of Congress
Cataloging-in-Publication Data

Falwell, Cathryn.
Turtle splash!: countdown at
the pond / by Cathryn Falwell.
p.   cm.
"Greenwillow Books."
Summary: As they are startled by the
activities of other nearby creatures,
the number of turtles on a log in a
pond decreases from ten to one.
ISBN: 978-0-06-029462-5 (trade bdg.)
ISBN: 978-0-06-029463-2 (lib. bdg.)
ISBN: 978-0-06-142927-9 (pbk.)
[1. Turtles—Fiction.
2. Counting. 3. Stories in rhyme.]
I. Title.   PZ8.3.F2163 Tu 2001
[E]—dc21   00-030918

11 12 13 SCP 20 19 18 17 16 15 14 13
First Edition

10

**Ten
timid turtles,
lounging
in a line.**

Startled by
a bullfrog ...

Then there
are nine.

9

Nine
napping turtles.
The day is
growing late.
A rabbit rustles
in the
leaves …

Now there
are eight.

8

Eight
lazy
turtles,
resting
without care.
A red squirrel
scampers
by the log ...

Seven still
are there.

7

Seven
sleepy turtles
hear the crunch
of sticks.
Deer appear
beside the
shore . . .

Now there
are six.

6

Six sunning
turtles, watching
ducklings dive.
The mother
mallard
quacks at
them …

Then there
are five.

5

Five
idle turtles,
lolling by
the shore.
Polliwogs
swirl by
their log . . .

Now there are four.

4

**Four
drowsy turtles,
quiet as can be.
A butterfly
flutters by ...**

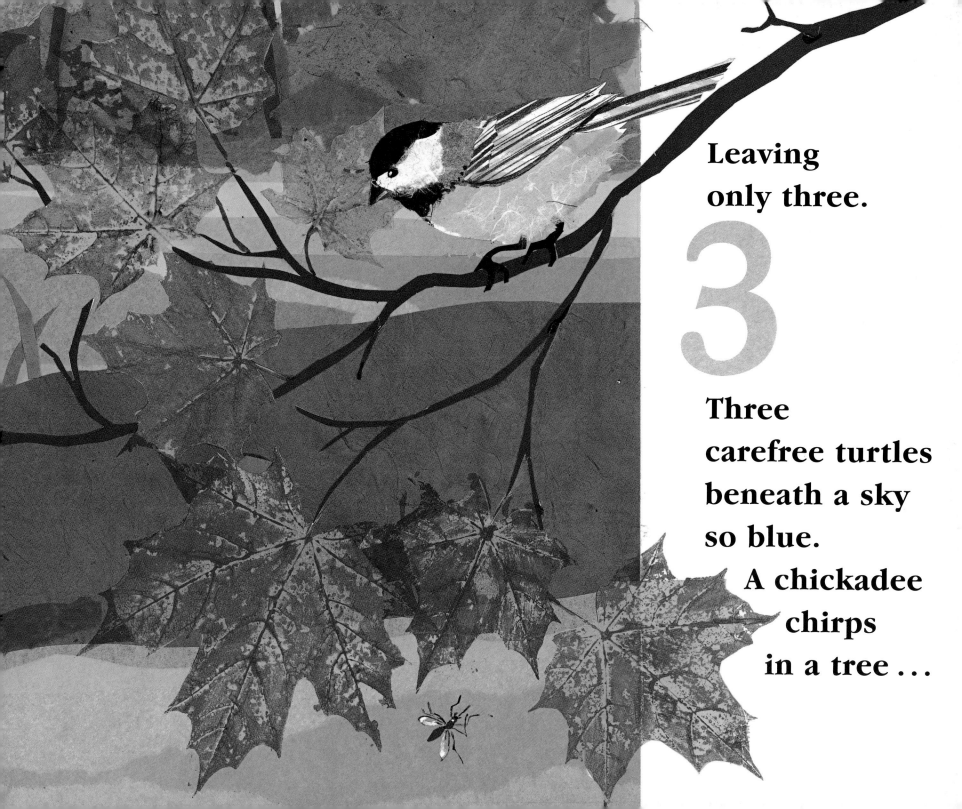

Leaving
only three.

3

Three
carefree turtles
beneath a sky
so blue.
A chickadee
chirps
in a tree . . .

Then there
are two.

2

Two
silent turtles
watch the
setting sun.
Mosquitoes
buzz above
their heads ...

Now there's
only one.

1

One
lonely turtle
in the fading
light . . .

Splash!

10

Ten
tired turtles
settle for
the night.

10
9
8
7
6
5
4
3
2
1

Sleep tight.

Life at the Pond

TURTLES

Eastern Painted Turtles have colorful designs on the edges of their shells and bodies. Although they are shy, they like to bask in the sun. At night they burrow in the mud underwater. Young turtles eat beetles and newly hatched insects, called larvae. Adult turtles eat mostly plants and also some insects and snails. An Eastern Painted Turtle can grow to be from 4" to 10" long.

BULLFROGS

In summer the bellows of bullfrogs can be heard booming across ponds. Bullfrogs choose special spots near the shore and will fight one another to protect their territories.

RABBITS

Cottontails line their nests with fur and grass to make them soft for their babies. They eat clover, seeds, grass, twigs, and fruits. Cottontails also like to eat vegetables from summer gardens. To avoid their enemies, cottontails jump and run fast zigzags. They are also very good swimmers.

SQUIRRELS

Small, chatty Red Squirrels eat mainly pinecone seeds but also nuts, bird eggs, buds, and fungi. They store lots of food for the winter. Their bushy tails help them keep their balance as they move quickly through the tree branches.

DEER

White-tailed Deer are shy animals that make their homes in the woods. Only the male, called a buck, has antlers. The female, called a doe, gives birth to one, two, or sometimes three babies, called fawns. A fawn's spotted coat helps it to hide in the leafy shadows beneath the trees.

DUCKS

Mallards are the most common ducks in the world. Male ducks are called drakes and females are called hens. They build their nests in tall grass near water. Fuzzy yellow and brown ducklings hatch from their eggs.

POLLIWOGS

Another name for polliwogs is tadpoles. Tadpoles are young frogs before they grow their legs. They have long, flat tails to help them swim. Bullfrog tadpoles take two or three years to grow into adult frogs.

BUTTERFLIES

The Great Spangled Fritillary, a large butterfly, lays eggs near violet plants. Spiky black-and-orange caterpillars hatch in late fall and spend the winter under dead leaves. In the spring these caterpillars feed on the new violet leaves before spinning chrysalises. Soon new butterflies will emerge from the chrysalises.

CHICKADEES

A small bird with a big voice, the Black-Capped Chickadee flies in a bobbing pattern. Chickadees eat caterpillars, moth eggs, beetles, and pinecone seeds. In winter chickadees will eat sunflower seeds from a bird feeder.

MOSQUITOES

These buzzing insects lay their eggs in or around still water. They get their food from flower nectar. Only the female mosquitoes bite, because they use blood for food when they are developing their eggs.

How to Make Leaf Prints

The illustrations for this book are collages made from a variety of materials that I cut and glued onto bristol board. The materials included handmade paper, tissue paper, grocery bags, construction paper, scraps saved from other projects, and small pieces of birch bark that I found on the ground. There are also leaf prints in the pictures. Here's a way to make leaf prints:

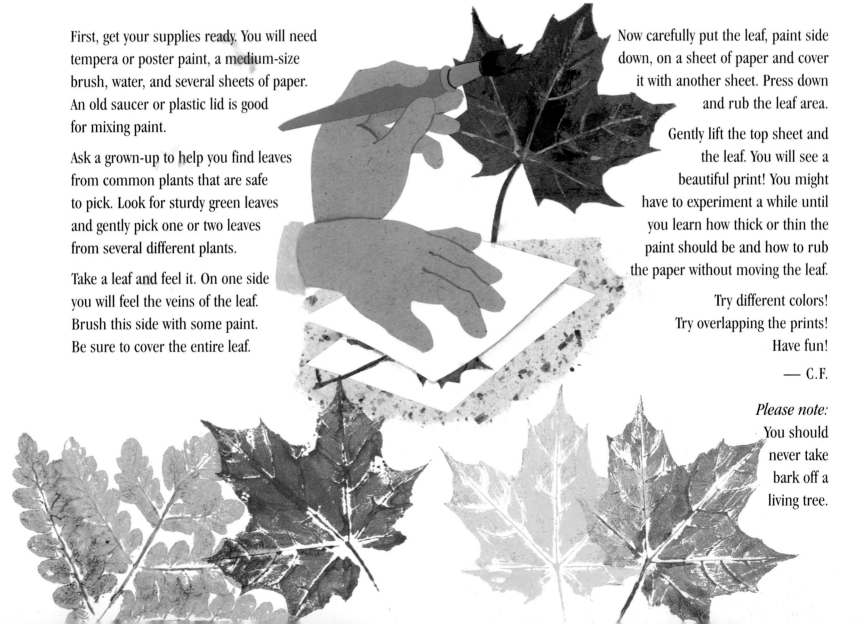

First, get your supplies ready. You will need tempera or poster paint, a medium-size brush, water, and several sheets of paper. An old saucer or plastic lid is good for mixing paint.

Ask a grown-up to help you find leaves from common plants that are safe to pick. Look for sturdy green leaves and gently pick one or two leaves from several different plants.

Take a leaf and feel it. On one side you will feel the veins of the leaf. Brush this side with some paint. Be sure to cover the entire leaf.

Now carefully put the leaf, paint side down, on a sheet of paper and cover it with another sheet. Press down and rub the leaf area.

Gently lift the top sheet and the leaf. You will see a beautiful print! You might have to experiment a while until you learn how thick or thin the paint should be and how to rub the paper without moving the leaf.

Try different colors!
Try overlapping the prints!
Have fun!

— C.F.

Please note:
You should never take bark off a living tree.